Dinosaur Chase

Dinosaur

by Carolyn Otto

Chase

illustrated by Thacher Hurd

HarperCollins Publishers

The hand lettering is by Donna Allman.

The pictures of the rocket ship and the baseball player on page 31 are by Nicholas Hurd.

The artwork was painted with india ink and transparent watercolors.

Dinosaur Chase
Text copyright © 1991 by Carolyn B. Otto
Illustrations copyright © 1991 by Thacher Hurd
Printed in the U.S.A. All rights reserved.
1 2 3 4 5 6 7 8 9 10
First Edition

Library of Congress Cataloging-in-Publication Data
Otto, Carolyn.
   Dinosaur chase / by Carolyn Otto ; illustrated by Thacher Hurd.
      p.   cm.
   Summary: A mother dinosaur reads her sleepy dinosaur son a bedtime story about a dinosaur chase that occurs when a precious necklace is stolen.
   ISBN 0-06-021613-1. — ISBN 0-06-021614-X (lib. bdg.)
   [1. Dinosaurs—Fiction. 2. Bedtime—Fiction.] I. Hurd, Thacher, ill. II. Title.
PZ7.O8794Di   1991   90-2021
[E]—dc20   CIP
                                                            AC

For KZ and PDH
C.B.O.

For Marilyn Marlow
T.H.

dinosaur two legs

dinosaur four

up there in the air
dinosaur soar

dinosaur swim

swish swish

dinosaur fishing

for dinosaur fish

dinosaur crawl
dinosaur creep

tiptoe dinosaur

dinosaur sneak

run run
dinosaur run

dinosaur chase
dinosaur race

hiding in

a dinosaur place

dinosaur snore

dream sweet
dinosaur dreams